FERAL

DEVILS POINT WOLVES #4

ELIZA GAYLE

GYPSY INK BOOKS

GET THE NEWS

Make sure you sign up for my newsletter for all the up-to-date book news, FREE books, and lots of behind the scenes goodies.

Sign up here: http://elizagayle.com/newsletter

PRO TIP: Make sure you add eliza@elizagayle.com to your contacts list to ensure the newsletter goes straight to your inbox.

ABOUT THE BOOK

Published by Gypsy Ink Books
© 2015 Eliza Gayle

eliza@elizagayle.com
http://ElizaGayle.com
Eliza on Instagram - elizagayleauthor
Eliza on Facebook - AuthorElizaGayle
Eliza on Tiktok - @elizagayleauthor

Sign up for Eliza's Newsletter -
elizagayle.com/newsletter

Book Description:

All it takes is one time...

Prue Davis is desperate. Her boss has gone nuts trying to show everyone his 'mangina', her research has been confiscated and her only hope of salvaging her career is to return to Devils Point and find out why so many wild wolves are drawn to one small island. She thinks she's prepared, but is anyone ever ready to find out their new lover is a werewolf?

Mating Season is over, but **Brody Fox is still going insane.** He's angry, resentful and probably dangerous. And he can't stop dreaming about the brown-eyed girl he wants to bite. Now he's ready to do or say anything to find the mate he lost. But if one more person calls him feral...

CHAPTER
ONE

rody stared out at the rocky beach from the inside of his tiny eight by eight cell unsure if he'd last another day in this hell hole. As far as holding cells went, this one wasn't so bad. The room was clean and he had a comfortable bed with plenty to eat.

None of which did a damn bit of good when the wolf inside him stirred constantly. If this is what it felt like to live with multiple personalities then those afflicted had his heartfelt sympathy because this shit sucked, keeping him on edge day and night.

The security detail assigned to watch over him kept calling him feral and he was sick and tired of hearing that too.

Several of the pack assured him he'd only be held here until they were certain he wasn't a danger to anyone else. But he knew better. In the midst of his frenzy he'd bitten an innocent girl, the mate to one of the pack leaders as it turned out. She survived, but that situation did not bode well for him and he knew it.

Not that he blamed them.

He spent his whole life hating and hunting down shapeshifters without ever understanding anything about them. Shifters called the hunters fanatics where Brody simply called them family.

Now, forced to walk in their skin it was easy to see just how narrow-minded he had been. Is that the way it always went? Hindsight and all that bullshit.

A growl formed deep in his throat. With the sun hidden behind the dark grey clouds, the outside seemed to match his inside as a storm continued to brew.

In the midst of his confusion after being accidentally bitten, the scent of a mate had given him hope and lured him to Devil's Point Island.

The disappearance of that scent had created a monster. One that refused to settle down no matter how hard he tried.

According to the pack living here on the island, his frenzy should have ended with mating season. The one time of year when all wolves go a little crazy with the need to find and bond with a mate. Only it didn't.

Weeks had passed and nothing changed. He still wanted to tear down the walls of his cell brick by brick and go on a hunt. Except he had no clue where to start.

The beautiful brown-haired girl he'd found on the beach had disappeared just as she appeared—without a trace.

After first scenting her in wolf form, he'd followed her scent for miles before finally coming upon her sitting on the beach in front of a campfire roasting marshmallows and laughing with her friends.

Night had fallen and the golden glow of the burning logs cast an ethereal aura around her. Instead of shifting and approaching her, he'd been a dumb ass and chosen to sit on his haunches and watch her from afar.

After traveling so long to catch her and not understanding the irresistible draw, he simply wanted to savor the moment.

He couldn't see the color of her eyes and had no idea what her name was, but in the soft light with the cool breeze blowing through his fur, none of that mattered.

Listening to her laugh with her scent wrapping around him calmed the chaos raging inside him. For the first time in weeks he'd felt a semblance of peace. Something even his human life never gave him.

Of course he'd been an idiot and waited too long. By the time he was ready to talk to her she'd disappeared into her tent and he didn't want to scare her by stalking her in her sleep.

Instead, he resigned himself to let them both get some rest before he approached her. He took cover in the tree line for the night and laid his body down in a soft spot of grass and fell asleep almost before his chin hit the ground.

When he woke she was gone. Somehow he'd slept through her departure and no amount of searching the island and surrounding areas had turned up even a trace of her.

He'd lost his *mate*.

His human side still balked at the idea of a fated mate. His sister, Allison, had been led down that path not long ago and now seemed somewhat settled with her new mate Diego.

She visited him everyday and he believed she might be happy if not for the worry lines that creased her forehead every time she saw him.

Brody pulled his gaze back from the beach and dropped to the floor and began doing push ups. Since he couldn't run free, he was forced to do calisthenics to ease some of the energy constantly overloading his system.

It didn't exactly work. But it made him almost civil so he continued to do it everyday.

Like every other day the number of reps flew by, sweat coated his body and his brain temporarily focused on the task at hand.

He wasn't thinking about anything beyond the determination to keep going so the new scent from the open window slammed into him unexpectedly.

Brody dropped and rolled, his hands ripping at the pants that confined his shift.

It couldn't be.

Before he registered what was happening claws tore at his zipper as he began to change and he barely got the denim off his legs before the bones popped and fur sprouted across his body.

He jumped on the window and inhaled deep, sticking his snout through the bars. It was there. The unmistakable scent of the woman never far from his mind.

No way.

The wolf began clawing at the walls below the window despite the fact the concrete construction gave him absolutely no way out.

He didn't care. All that mattered was getting to the woman he needed more than anything else. He scratched and scraped until his forearms ached and his claws were worn down to the quick.

"Brody, what the hell are you doing?"

The wolf jerked at the sound of his sister's voice behind him, giving his human half a chance to regain control. As quickly as he shifted to wolf, he changed back.

"Holy shit." Allison jerked away from him and turned her back. "Give a girl some warning. I do not need to see your junk—Ever!"

He looked down at his nudity and almost smiled. Any other time he would have teased her mercilessly about being so squeamish. Not today. Not when the answer to his prayers stood right in front of him.

"Allison, you've got to get me out of here." He grabbed his pants and shoved his legs in them, barely taking the two seconds to fasten the zipper and button.

"You know I can't do that." She sighed. "How many times are we going to go over this? It's not safe. "

"For who?" he growled. "Me? You?"

"The whole pack, Brody. This isn't just about you and me anymore. There's a lot more at stake."

He rolled his eyes and groaned. "I can't believe how easily you accepted the whole pack mentality. What happened to bucking the system? Being an individual? Not being a sheep?"

"Because we're not human anymore," she hissed. "Wolves need the pack."

"So you've said."

"I'm not the only one," she retorted. "Don't discount what Diego and his brothers have to say. They've dealt with ferals before."

He cringed at the word. The fact even his sister called him that did not give him much of a chance. But he had to try.

"Have they ever saved a feral? It would seem our captors don't say much about that."

"We aren't captives."

He looked around his small room. "Really? I know I can't go anywhere. Are you so sure you can? What if you wanted to leave the island?"

"Don't be ridiculous. I chose this life. I chose Diego and I'm happier for it. Can't you understand that? We just need to stick together. All of us. The pack."

He stepped forward and leaned against the plexiglass that separated them. "If that's true then how am I supposed to be getting better being isolated in here? It's impossible to acclimate in isolation."

She shook her head. "I'm not letting you out. Not until Diego says it's safe."

Brody banged his hand on the clear divider. "Don't be like this, Sis. I'm not trying to get free so I can go on some insane killing spree. Being locked up is the problem. I just want..." He stopped, unable to say the words even to his sister.

"You want what?" Suspicion rose in her voice.

He considered his next words carefully. He didn't like having to manipulate her, but he was desperate. No way in hell he'd lose the woman on the beach twice.

"There's a woman. I can smell her."

Allison crunched up her face. "Eww, seriously? I don't want to hear this."

"Oh for fuck's sake. I am not talking about sex. She is far more important than that. It's the mate bond." He swallowed down the distaste of his lies. But he had to do something...

"We connected during mating season before I understood what was happening. She was here on vacation, but by the time I realized the true nature of what she was to me she'd left the island."

Allison's stance and features were softening as he spoke. The curse of someone in love is that they want everyone around them to be in love too. It made his sister easy prey.

"I saw her on the beach this morning. She's returned and I think she's pregnant with my baby."

Her hand flew to her mouth. "How can you be so sure?"

He tapped his nose. "Heightened senses, baby. This thing tells me all kinds of stuff now."

She nodded, obviously agreeing with him.

"So you see? You have to help me get out of here so I can find her. I can't let my pregnant mate suffer."

Suddenly the sound of clapping filled his small cell and Creed, one of the men keeping any eye on him, walked out of the shadows.

"Wow. That was quite a performance. That's some serious balls you've got there to feed that bullshit to your sister though."

Allison's face hardened and her eyes narrowed. "Is that what you were doing? Lying to me to get what you wanted?"

When he didn't immediately answer she stomped her foot and exited the room without another word.

"Thanks, bro," Brody muttered.

Creed smiled back at him. "I don't think she was going to let you out anyway. Diego would have given her hell and probably tried to lock her up again."

"What do you mean again?"

He shrugged. "They didn't exactly meet under the best of circumstances. Before he figured out what to do with her he had to detain her somehow."

Brody shook his head. "Let me guess. It didn't work."

"Nope," Creed paused. "I heard she got herself free in less than ten minutes."

"That's my sister. The escape artist."

"Too bad you didn't get that trait. Maybe you wouldn't be making up strange stories to get loose."

"It wasn't all lies," Brody said. "I did sort of meet a woman during mating season."

"And? Don't leave a brother hanging. Mating season is a kick ass time for us unattached wolves. For some it means finding the elusive true mate. As for the rest of us, we just want to screw every available woman who will have us. "

Brody had to fight the urge to lash out at Creed. As much as he respected the man for his loyalty to the pack and the respect he gave him, he didn't like his mystery woman being lumped in with the conquests he and Sawyer bragged about.

"It wasn't like that. There was—I don't know—something about her scent that made me feel different."

"No shit. Are you serious?"

Brody lifted his shoulders. "Like I said. No big deal."

"Uh huh. Did her scent make you desperate to get close to her? Or did you feel unusually settled when you were around her?"

Yes. It was exactly like that, but he didn't like the direction Creed was headed. He didn't want to talk about their mating crap anymore.

"I wouldn't know. Before I could talk to her I got a text from Allison that she was on the island looking for me. I took cover and by the time I made it back to the beach, the woman was gone."

The other man nodded. "I knew you were bullshitting Allison. She is going to kick your ass."

"Probably. If I ever get out of here that is. Not a whole lot she can do with me in here and her out there." He was really fighting the need to snarl at Creed by this point. The scent of the woman on the beach was making the damned wolf insane, beating at his brain.

"Was anything you said real? Or are you bullshitting me too? I've got a much better nose for lies than your newbie sister."

"I caught her scent again." His words were clipped as the aggression in him rose.

"And you need to get out there, don't you? The wolf is riding your ass to do something and do something quick."

He nodded, gritting his teeth. "How do you know? You aren't mated. Not that I'm putting a lot of stock in that nonsense."

Creed reached into his pocket and pulled out his keys. "That's a story for another day." He slid the metal into the cell lock and opened the door.

"Don't make me regret this. If you pull something stupid I will put you down and then I'm going to be really pissed."

Brody failed to see how his logic worked, but he didn't care. The only thing standing between him and freedom was this one shifter. And he was willing to tell him anything he wanted to hear if it meant he got what he wanted.

"You won't regret it. Unless you keep toying with me. Then we'll both have regrets."

TWO

P rue Davis dug her toes into the sand and looked out over the rocky shoreline. A light breeze ruffled her long hair and the salty ocean scent calmed her nerves.

It would be summer soon and she imagined the beach filled with families from all over the country. The Pacific Northwest was idyllic in the summer and it drew people from many states that were desperate to escape the oppressive summer heat.

Not that she blamed them. As far as she was concerned this part of the country suited her perfectly. Her job in Montana had been the perfect position at the right time, but ever since spring break, this island and her research had been calling out to her.

At least that's what she spent half her day convincing herself. It was easier to say that her return trip to Devil's Point Island was all about her life's work versus the cold hard truth.

She'd lost her job and possibly ruined her chances at another. At least as a wildlife biologist. The bitterness that had been eating away at her for the last several weeks roared up and threatened to consume her once again.

It was hard to not feel sorry for herself when her only crime had been being in the wrong place at the wrong time. She closed her eyes at the onslaught of memories. Once upon a time she was on the fast track for a spectacular career under the tutelage of renowned wildlife researcher and longtime professor John Mahoney.

And then he went nuts.

Not a little crazy. He couldn't be like the other nutty professors with their eccentric episodes that could be chalked up to stress. Nope. John took the full-blown psychotic crazy route with the aid of twelve-year scotch.

Right after returning from spring break she attended one of the university fundraisers that was set to fund their Pacific Northwest wolf conservation and relocation program. To her shock, all it had taken was a cheating wife and a bottle of booze to obliterate her dreams.

Of course John couldn't be garden variety when it came to his breakdown. Oh no...

Instead of an alcohol bender and some sort of fight that might have landed him in jail for twenty-four hours to sleep it off like a normal person, he got drunk at the party. Then proceeded to take all his clothes off, stand on the bar and tuck his penis between his legs and launch into a long, slurred speech about the stupidity of researching wildlife when we don't even understand the humans and supernatural currently living among us.

She shook her head. It had taken three big bodyguards to drag his ass down and off campus. Needless to say, he was not going to be teaching students or heading any more research projects anytime soon.

And in her case—no professor, no assistant position. She was let go effective immediately and who in their right mind wanted to hire a biologist associated with a very public scandal?

She stabbed her foot into the sand.

Nobody, that's who. As evidenced by her deathly silent cell phone and university after university declining to interview her for so much as a janitorial position.

Although it was her recent research that took the biggest hit. Her findings from her spring break trip were confiscated and her computers with all of her data seized by the university.

Which was a round about but direct way of saying that's how she ended up here. The small island that after one night of camping on the beach had stuck in her brain.

Rumors of the island having an unusually large pack of wolves had her suspicious and under the guise of a backpacking trip with friends, she'd come here to gather any evidence of said wolves and what might have drawn them to such a small territory of a mere two hundred and sixty acres.

Then there was the lone wolf from this beach...

She couldn't shake the memory of the wolf hovering in the tree line watching her. His behavior had struck her odd and she wanted to know more.

Of course he might have been stalking the group for some sort of attack, but she doubted it. Its body language had not seemed primed for an attack.

Prue wiped the hair out of her eyes. Maybe *she* was going crazy. Thinking that a wolf was watching her like she was something other than prey sounded pretty stupid even in her own mind.

"Hi there."

Prue twisted to the female voice behind her and found a pretty blonde coming up behind her.

"Hello," she answered cautiously. She wasn't really up for idle chit chat with a stranger. This was supposed to be her "feel sorry for myself" whinefest and she was gearing up for a pretty big pity party later that evening.

"I hear there's a storm brewing. You might want to head back to the mainland before the bridge washes out." The woman plopped down in the sand next to her. "I mean I wouldn't want you to get stranded here with nothing to do and nowhere to go. What with the lack of amenities for hu—uh—people."

Prue shrugged, eying the woman warily. "I could always take shelter in the club by the bridge."

The woman laughed. "I didn't take you for the stripper club kind of person."

Prue looked down at her ragged, thread bare tank top and tattered jeans that had definitely seen better days, but made her ridiculously comfortable. "I guess you're right. I'm not exactly dressed the part, huh?"

The woman snorted. "If you think the guys in there would care one iota how you are dressed you couldn't be more wrong. They won't be able to see past your boobs."

Prue scrunched up her face at the image that put in her brain. Perverts in a dark club drooling over mostly naked women. *Yuck.*

"Yeah, no thanks."

The stranger laughed and stuck out her hand. "I'm Allison by the way. I live here on the island."

Prue took her hand and was pleasantly surprised to find she had a firm, trustworthy handshake. Nothing was as bad as meeting a woman and shaking a limp hand. It gave her the creeps. "Prue Davis," she answered. "I don't live here obviously."

"What brings you to our humble little island? Vacation?"

She studied Allison for a moment and wondered how much to tell her. It seemed a little odd that she popped out of nowhere and was now grilling her for a life story.

"Yeah. A little getaway. I was here several months ago on a backpacking trip and I guess the place stuck with me." She lifted her shoulders. "So I'm back."

"You got a room at the motel? I noticed this morning we were full."

The unease crawling up Prue's back thickened. She had no idea why this woman was being so nosy about her, but it made her uncomfortable.

She stood and wiped the sand from her pants legs and butt. "No, I didn't really think that far ahead. So maybe you're right and I should leave."

Allison's face dropped. "I'm sorry I didn't mean to offend you. We don't get as many travelers as you might think and it's a tiny island. You know, the kind of place where everyone knows everything about everybody. An unfamiliar face not here for the Diablo is especially rare."

Some of the tension eased from Prue during Allison's small speech. Maybe she was being a little paranoid thanks to her recent scandal. "That's too bad. About the lack of visitors I mean. The view is amazing from here. A lot better than watching some poor girl trying to put herself through college by grasping onto a pole and gyrating her way through the night."

Allison broke out in a fit of giggles so infectious they made Prue laugh too. Maybe she was overthinking this situation. Just because a stranger wanted to chat with her didn't mean there was some sinister reason.

"So if there's no where to spend the night other than my tent, can you recommend somewhere on the island I could get some food? I'm suddenly starving."

"Well," Allison hesitated. "You could go to the diner. Or you could go to the diner. It's all we've got."

Prue smiled. "Okay you've convinced me. The diner it is."

A whistle sounded from the tree line and both women turned to look. To Prue's surprise there were three men standing among the trees watching them.

Three tall and gorgeous men from what she could tell. They may have been dressed casual in jeans and T-shirts, but they could have been wearing anything and looked damned fine doing it.

Two of them had dark hair and similar scowls stamped across their face, but it was the one in the middle who drew her attention. Sandy brown hair curled around his ears, highlighting the chiseled cheek bones in a square jaw that somehow exuded the kind of manly power that took her breath away and sent tingles of sensation trickling down her arms and legs.

He was beautiful.

"Busy place," Prue mumbled.

Allison waved to the men and one of them pointed to his wrist as if indicating time.

"Yours I take it?"

The woman turned her attention back to Prue. "Yeah, I guess so."

Her words were vague but the big smile on her face spoke volumes. She was in love with at least one of those men. Maybe more. These days you couldn't make assumptions.

She bent down and scooped up her backpack and settled it on her back. "I think that's my cue to get going. It was nice meeting you, Allison. Maybe we'll run into each other again. I might be here a while."

The young woman stilled and slowly turned to face her. "Oh yeah? Why is that?"

"Because I'm here to study the wolves."

THREE

Brody could hardly hold himself back from the woman standing on the beach talking to his sister. The wolf inside him wanted to go to her and take what he needed despite any cost. Fortunately his human side still maintained control most of the time and he stayed rooted to the spot like a good little dog.

"Your sister is a handful," Creed said.

Both Diego and Brody growled at him. It didn't matter that he was pretty annoyed at Allison at the moment. Those thoughts and comments were reserved for him. Maybe Diego, since his sister had become his mate during the last mating season.

Creed held up his hands. "What? I'm just saying what I know you both were thinking."

Brody shook his head and turned back to the two women on the beach. "She's always been like that. Growing up she never listened. The best way to get her to do something is to tell her she can't. It's the ultimate motivation for her."

"So who is this woman?" Diego asked.

"Don't know. Last time I saw her I didn't get a chance to speak to her before she left. You and Allison were on my ass."

Creed snorted. "I can't believe that you—"

Diego and Brody growled at the same time to shut him up, their focus entirely on the two women. He didn't know exactly what they were talking about other than a few snatches of words on the wind, but his sister had gone on alert. Her body language now screamed danger and it offended the wolf.

Diego marched out of the trees, headed for his woman. He and Creed followed. Brody kept his eyes on his mystery woman the whole time.

Something was wrong.

He scented fear from both Allison and the other woman. Curious. He saw no threat in the vicinity or scented anything out of the ordinary.

Diego reached them first and he pulled Allison against his side and wrapped his arm around her. He also pressed a quick kiss against her forehead and whispered in her ear. Allison nodded.

All this Brody saw from his peripheral vision, as he had not taken his eyes from the woman who still stared at the sand.

"Prue, this is my husband, Diego."

Brody felt more than he saw Diego stiffen slightly at Allison's use of the human term. They weren't legally wed, only mated. To Diego's credit he recovered quickly and Brody doubted the woman named Prue even noticed.

Prue.

He rolled the name back and forth in his head, allowing it to filter through his senses. Unusual and uncommon. He liked that. Although he really didn't like the fact that Diego was still touching her. His eyes narrowed and an all too familiar red haze began filling his vision.

As much as he wanted to deny what the pack kept warning him about, these bouts of inexplicable rage were not easy to control or push back.

Allison must have sensed his agitation as she acted quickly by turning to him. "And this is my brother, Brody."

Finally his mystery woman turned his way and their gazes met, making him forget for a moment that some other man had been too close to his woman.

Instead a pure moment of sizzling energy rushed down his spine making him swallow the need to lift his head and howl.

Up close he spotted the dark green flecks of her brown eyes and the small smattering of freckles across her button nose and the long inky lashes that fluttered against her skin every few seconds.

His body grew taut as he drank her in. He couldn't have looked away from her if there was a bomb going off in his vicinity. That's how entranced he was by this woman.

He stepped forward and took her hand. The energy already surging through him sparked and both their bodies jerked. Her eyes widened and her pulse sped up as he gently squeezed her hand and held onto it.

Mine.

The word repeated in his mind, making sure that he knew exactly what the wolf wanted and that he was going to get it whether he liked it or not.

"Prue," he said. Not really asking a question just wanting to say her name again.

"Yep." She gently pulled her hand from his and looked away from him. Turning to Allison she said, "I think I really should go now. I've got some work to do."

The hair on Brody's nape rose at the change in Diego's demeanor. It was weird how his wolf senses came out often even while in human form. Sometimes it surprised him and others it turned out damned convenient.

"What kind of work do you have here on the island?"

Not liking the steel in Diego's tone, Brody inched closer to Prue and angled his body so he was slightly in front of her and in a position to protect her if need be.

"I'm studying some plants here on the island. I think they might be affecting the wildlife in an unusual way."

Brody squeezed his eyebrows together. He wasn't getting why Allison and Diego seemed so concerned about Prue. What did it matter if she was interested in some sort of silly plant?

"How so?" Diego asked, taking the words out of Brody's mouth.

"There have been a lot of reports lately about increased wolf sightings in this area. Enough that I got curious and came here back in the spring looking for something that might be the cause."

"You study wolves?" Brody asked, unsure how that information was going to play out all things considered.

She turned to him, nodding. "I'm a wildlife biologist so I actually study many animals, but in this case, yes. I want to study the wolf patterns in this area.

"Unfortunately, this is private property." This time it was Creed who spoke up and his abrupt outburst did not sit well with Brody.

A faint blush crawled up Prue's neck. "I thought it was open to tourists. I camped here a few months ago and gathered some data. I only need a little more to finish."

Diego shook his head. "Probably not a good idea. If we've got an overpopulation of wolves, as you suggest, then you need to be careful. Plus there's a storm brewing."

"It really would only take me a few minutes. If I can prove that the unusual plant life of the island is attracting the wild wolves then our scientists can use that research in their quest to repopulate certain species of wolves that have been dying out and place them in more appropriate areas." She was shuffling her feet and pulling at the edge of her shirt. Her display of nerves said more than the words. This was obviously important to her for more reasons than she mentioned.

"Who do you work for?"

Her face blanked for a minute and her eyes darted past the men standing in front of her. He had a feeling she was about to take off on them and he couldn't let that happen.

Let her run.

The wolf had different ideas. Apparently the thought of a chase was his idea of fun.

"I don't work for anyone at the moment."

Diego and Creed frowned. "You said our scientists. Who is our?"

Diego had an incredible memory for detail. He retained things others didn't.

"Well..." She looked at the ground. "Just a general figure of speech?" The fact her answer came out a question made it obvious to them all she was lying.

"Nice try. Now tell us the truth." Diego demanded harshly.

Brody growled and both Diego and Creed turned their attention to him.

"What's wrong?" Creed asked him.

Brody didn't answer right away. There were some things that weren't supposed to be discussed in front of humans. "Nothing."

Creed narrowed his eyes and compressed his lips together, his obvious detection of the lie all over his face.

"Don't do—"

"So who do you work for?" Diego asked Prue, cutting off Creed from whatever he'd been about to say.

She sighed, a harsh breath expelling from her lungs. "Maybe I should talk to whoever owns the island. I can assure him that I can complete my research without being intrusive."

"You've got him," Diego said. "Me and my family anyways."

"Okaaay," She said, her eyes nice and wide. "I wasn't lying. It is true that I don't work for anyone at the moment. I recently lost my job. But that's a long story I'd rather not get into. However, I am hoping that with positive results to prove my hypothesis I might be able to secure a position at Wolf Haven. They're a wolf sanctuary a couple of hours from here."

"I'm familiar. Although that doesn't really influence me in letting you roam our island and disturb the residents. We value our privacy here."

Prue's eyes narrowed and Brody swore he saw a spark in her eye. Things were about to go seriously south.

"Is that why you have a strip club? So no one will come here and check you out. That seems a little rich to encourage tourists to partake in your young girls, and then deny a scientist some simple research that has no bearing whatsoever on your 'residents' She held up her hands and made air quotes to emphasis her point and Brody had to bite his tongue to keep from laughing out loud.

Diego on the other hand looked ready to blow. Allison must have sensed it too as she did what she always did best and calmed him by placing her hand on her arm. "What's the harm in allowing her to take some plant samples, Romeo?"

Brody winced. Diego didn't always appreciate Allison's incessant need to call him by a nickname she gave him before they were mated.

"Don't like strangers."

"She's not." Brody stood straighter. "I met her last time she was on the island and I'll vouch for her if you need me to."

Prue shifted behind him. "I don't—"

Brody reached behind him and grabbed her hip and squeezed. She squeaked but also stopped talking.

"I thought you didn't know her?"

He shrugged. "Well enough to know she's harmless. That's all that matters right?"

Silence descended as Diego thought over what he said. Creed stayed silent. He'd already gone out on a limb by releasing him and didn't need to do more that could blow up in his face. Brody preferred to have this on his shoulders if something went wrong.

He glanced back at the woman he'd searched high and low for and willed her to keep quiet. It must have worked because she didn't say another word.

When Diego finally spoke, they were all wound as tight as could be. "She'll need an escort if she goes anywhere other than the public beaches or the club."

"I'll do it," Brody blurted.

Everyone spoke at once. Prue, Creed and Allison all had their own opinion on that idea.

"Enough," Diego ordered.

Brody bristled at his tone. He and his brothers might lead this pack, but that didn't mean Brody was ready to roll over and automatically obey. Wolf or not, that behavior was absolutely not in his DNA.

"A word." Diego said, indicating with a tilt of his head that both Creed and Brody were to follow him. "Excuse us."

Allison stayed with Prue while he, Creed and Diego walked through the sand until they were out of earshot. Or at least human earshot. Allison would hear everything they said.

"What the hell is going on here?" Diego asked.

"I think he's got a nut for the woman."

"I'm right here," Brody said, not appreciating Creed's assessment.

"That true?" Diego asked.

He shook his head. "I don't know. Maybe I just need to get laid." He maintained a straight face when he said it because he didn't want to go into the details of his torment all these months. That was none of their God damned business.

"I don't like it. Having a human poking around the island sounds like a bad idea."

"And what the hell is she talking about that a certain plant is drawing wolves here? What kind of craziness is that?" Creed interjected.

"Sounds like nonsense," Brody agreed. "But what does it hurt to indulge her?"

"That part about the plant isn't totally untrue." Diego's voice lowered.

Creed looked as confused as Brody felt.

Diego smiled. "We've been here a long time, things have happened. Many forgotten."

"Don't talk cryptic bullshit and tell us what she's talking about." Creed sounded on edge.

"Supposedly the origin of the name Devil's Point comes from a plant that used to grow here in abundance called Devil's Club. Now it's not as prevalent as we've learned to control it."

Brody smirked. "What is this? The little island of horrors?"

Diego ignored his sarcasm. "The berries that grow on them are rumored to have many useful properties to shapeshifters."

"Like what?" Brody asked. He was beginning to not like the sound of this.

"They were mostly used for medicinal purposes before modern medicine rendered them unnecessary."

"And?"

"And the berries are also filled with pheromones that act as an aphrodisiac to some shifters, particularly wolves."

"How come I don't know anything about these berries? Where are they?" asked Creed.

Diego shrugged. "Over the years as we populated the island, they began dying out. They are around here and there but not in a large enough quantity that you'd ever notice."

"And you think that's what Prue found on her last visit here? One of those bushes and now she's looking for more?"

Diego shrugged. "Sounds like it. Except we all know that has nothing to do with the reason there are so many wolves on this island. I'd sure like to know where she got data on that. If we have a leak or someone is keeping an eye on us, I need to know about it."

Creed nodded. "Agreed."

"Then let her stay so we can find out. What difference does it make if she finds any of these plants? If it doesn't mean anything? I'll stay with her and make sure she doesn't wander anywhere she shouldn't."

"You really think you can handle that on your first day of freedom?" Diego asked.

"I'm fine. I haven't felt the urge to bite anyone in quite some time." Except in his dreams that featured one brown eyed girl he now knew was named Prue. He always wanted to bite her.

Creed turned to Diego. "Let him do it. He's ready."

Diego stayed silent for several long seconds. "Fine. But you're responsible for both of them. If something goes wrong it's on your head."

Creed smirked. "Got it, boss. My head on a chopping block. Wouldn't be the first time, right?"

Diego grinned and clapped Creed on the back. "I guess not. You always seem to find trouble."

As the two men joked with each other, Brody worked on calming the wolf inside him. It felt as if he was going to burst out of his skin at any moment and go after the woman.

What was his deal? Why was this woman so important?

He turned back to the two women waiting on the beach and began walking toward them. Each step making it harder for him to control the wolf. As much as he wanted to spend time with her, he hated not being in total control.

"So?" Allison asked. "What's the verdict?"

"You've been granted escorted access." Brody looked at Prue as he spoke. He was definitely ready for the rest of them to leave.

"Told you Diego was a softie." Allison smiled.

"I heard that." Diego yanked Allison against his front and banded his arms around her. "Does any of that feel soft to you?"

She smiled and shook her head.

"Ugh." Brody turned away from the implied meaning of Diego's words and grabbed Prue's hand. "How about we get out of here before watching this brute maul my sister in public makes me ill or lose my temper."

Prue gave him a small smile and nodded. He grabbed her backpack from the ground and hefted it over his shoulder. "Good night, what do you have in this thing?"

She giggled, a sweet soft sound that made his body tighten further. Not that he wasn't already half hard just from sight and scent alone.

"My ancient laptop is ridiculously heavy I know. Want me to take it?"

He didn't bother to respond but he must have made a funny face because she started to laugh again. He tugged her hand and began leading her away from the group. Creed had an odd look on his face and Brody wanted to get the hell out of there before any of them changed their minds about him.

"Stay away from the residential areas," Diego ordered. "I don't need to get any phone calls today."

Brody lifted his hand and saluted. "Yes, Sir." He tried to temper his sarcasm around any of the alphas but it wasn't easy. He had always balked at being told what to do. Taking orders definitely went against his nature. Something he didn't know how he'd reconcile while living with a pack.

CREED WATCHED Brody lead the human woman away. There was something about the way Brody suffered that rang a little too close to home. The anger always sitting just below the surface spoke to something different than simply turning feral. There was an underlying reason and he was pretty sure it had something to do with this woman.

"You really think that was a good idea?"

He turned to Diego. "I think it had to be done."

"You know what's going to happen right?"

"Yes. I'm well aware of the effect a newly turned wolf has on a human. But I think there's something else going on he doesn't understand yet and his wolf might be the only one he'll listen to."

Diego shook his head. "We're playing with fire on this one. Anything goes wrong and it's going to blow up in our face. Not to mention his little scientist might draw a lot of unwanted attention to our private island. We definitely don't need that."

"Trust me," Creed said. "I don't think it's going to come to that. She's going to be sufficiently distracted from her fact finding mission."

"What are you his pimp now? You think getting him laid is going to solve all his problems?"

Creed looked at him, a gold glint of the wolf showing in his eyes.

"It solved yours didn't it?

FOUR

Prue tried to think about something else besides the big, strong hand wrapped around hers. His first touch had caused tingles to erupt across her body and she hadn't quite recovered.

At the moment he was in front of her leading the way up the beach, which gave her a spectacular rear view of the handsome man. His broad shoulders flexed and moved under his shirt making her wonder what they would feel like under her fingers.

More tingles erupted along her spine as her gaze traveled south to the tapered waist and tight butt that she watched mesmerized as he moved.

What the hell was wrong with her? Yes, he was gorgeous. Yes, he appeared to have a perfect hot body.

But, it's not as if she hadn't seen that before. So why did she want to reach out and squeeze him?

She shook her head, trying to clear it of her crazy thoughts as they entered the wooded trail that led back to the main road. When they reached the clearing he stopped and turned back to her, still gripping her hand.

"So where to, Professor?" he asked.

"I'm not a professor, just a researcher. I'm a long way from having my teaching credentials."

He smiled down on her, looking wholly amused. He took a step closer to her and she held her breath. His hand came up and brushed some of her hair out of her eyes. "It doesn't matter if you're a bonafide professor or not, Professor. You've got the whole beautiful geeky thing going on that makes me think of you as a hot teacher. That's what counts."

Prue blinked, startled by his brazen words. Beautiful geek? Half of her wanted to be affronted and the other nearly swooned.

"Do you have a thing for teachers? Is that what this is about?" she asked.

He laughed again. "I never thought so, but I think I just changed my mind. If they look as sexy as you do, then yeah I've got a thing for them."

She shook her head. "Good thing I'm not a teacher then."

As soon as she quit talking his fingertip touched her bottom lip. "It doesn't really matter when I've already got the perfect image of you in my head."

A shiver worked down her spine at the gentle caress. The man touching her was a virtual stranger and she was oddly drawn to him. So much so that it would be easy to forget why she was here and the job she had to do. So much of her life had been focused on academia and then research that it left zero time for a social life.

How long had it been since she'd had a date? She couldn't remember. But here with his eyes focused on her and his fingers stroking her face, it seemed suddenly important.

"I'm not perfect," she whispered. "Far from it."

"Not from where I'm standing." He gripped her bicep and tugged her close. They weren't touching, but she could feel the body heat emanating from him.

"I see perfect eyes. A perfect nose. And perfect lips I want nothing more than to taste."

Prue tried to breath through the shock of need coursing through her. Her panties were wet at the mere thought of this man kissing her. And she wanted it. She wanted it bad.

"You don't know me."

He smiled, a gentle change softening his hard features and he backed away slowly. "Fair enough for now. So how about we fix that? Tell me something about Prue Davis. Where are you from?"

"Montana," she said on a shaky breath.

"Never been," he said. "What's it like there?"

Prue tried to form an answer in her head when all she could focus on was the man standing right in front of her staring her down. His interest seemed genuine, but so did the hunger. It was stamped across his face.

"It's really cold in the winter, but the summers are amazing. Like Washington, there is so much to do outdoors and the wildlife is incredible."

He crossed his arms, giving her a scrumptious view of his forearms and biceps. Each were highlighted with cords of muscle and tan skin with a light coating of fine hairs that she wanted to run her fingers across.

"Is that what got you interested in wolves?"

"What?" She shook her head to gain some focus. "Oh yeah. My father was an outdoorsman. Spent all his free time either hunting or fishing. As the only child, I often went with him. Although I hated the killing, I gained a surprising respect for nature and all its intricacies from him."

Brody nodded his head. "So now you try to save the wild animals instead of kill them. Interesting."

A different kind of shudder worked down Prue's back as she recalled one particular hunting trip that changed her life forever. There were rules that always had to be followed to the letter her father always said. And usually Prue did as she was told.

Except that one time. Earlier in the day they'd come across a nearby campsite of young college boys who her father was not happy to find partying in his woods. After a brief lecture about safety they'd gone down stream and set up camp a ways away.

Unfortunately, the college guys had caught her curiosity and she'd snuck off late in the night to get a closer look. Since the boys had not listened to any of her father's suggestions, she wasn't the only one who went looking.

Not far from their pitched tents, she'd come across a hungry grizzly bear. In a panic, Prue had forgotten her father's bear rules and she'd run and the bear, thinking she was prey, gave chase.

She squeezed her eyes closed and shut down the memory before it got worse. It had taken years to sleep through the night after her father's death and a trip down memory lane would not help her now.

"I owe everything to my father. He taught me all that I know."

Brody's face tightened as she talked. His body language stiffened too. God, if only she had more experience with men like him. Or any men really she might be able to understand him better.

"My father taught me everything I know too. Unfortunately, I don't think it had the same results. He has a lot of hate in his heart and it's only recently I came to my senses. I had to make some drastic changes that landed me here."

Her resolve to stick to business and not get involved with anyone began to thaw. She reached out and grabbed his hand, this time embracing the electric spark that sizzled up her arm and spread through her chest.

"What about your sister? Allison, right? She seems friendly."

His lips curved in a small smile. "She's great. Stubborn, opinionated and spoiled now thanks to Diego. But yeah, she's great."

She squeezed his fingers. "I always thought it would be fun to have a sibling. Someone to share the good and the bad."

"It might be overrated."

He sounded serious, but she didn't believe him for a second. The affection in his voice when he talked about his sister made it clear they were close. She got the feeling though, he'd been in a lot of pain lately. Something really bad had to have happened to turn him away from the rest of his family.

"Why did you stick up for me back there?" she asked. "You made your friends seem like you knew me. But you don't know me at all. Certainly not enough to vouch for me."

He shrugged. "Call it a hunch."

He didn't expand his explanation and she got the feeling there was more he wanted to say.

"Thank you," she whispered. "It's been a long time since anyone has been so nice."

He reached out and touched the side of her face. "That's a shame. You deserve so much more."

Prue cocked her head and tried to read between the lines of his words by staring at his eyes. She could swear they were lighter now. More golden around the edge of the pupil than before.

"Why would you say that? How do you know I'm not a mass murderer who is going to go on a rampage after dark?"

His thumb moved back and forth across her cheek. "Are you?"

She swallowed, willing the lump in her throat to go away. "No, I guess not."

"Just because you aren't used to someone being nice to you doesn't mean you don't deserve it," he said.

"Shouldn't that go both ways?" Who was this gorgeous enigma of a man, who despite not knowing her very long, inspired her to not only feel comfortable with him, but also trust him? How was that possible?

"Eventually." He leaned forward and pressed a light kiss to the top of her ear. "Although my only concern is you and your pleasure."

Her arousal spiked hard with his heated breath tickling her sensitive ear. A shiver worked up her back and goose bumps broke out on her arms.

"You're making it really hard for me to concentrate on my job right now."

"Am I?" he whispered while trailing his fingers down the sides of her neck to her shoulders. "I'd rather be touching you."

Prue moaned. "So not fair."

"Fair is overrated," he said with a smile.

"It's a good thing you are hot or I'd have an issue with you right now. But still, we're going plant hunting before I lose my control along with my panties."

Prue hoisted her backpack from the ground where it had slid and settled it on her shoulder. "Lead the way, lover boy."

"You think I'm hot."

Brody's statement stopped her cold. Was he serious? She didn't know what to say, but for some reason it was so... She doubled over and started laughing. Not a soft peal of laughter. Of course not. This was full on belly laugh that made her sound like a stupid hyena. And it felt good.

By the time she recovered she had streams of tears running down her face and he was standing there staring at her with an equally goofy grin.

Her heart melted.

"I guess we should look for plants," he said. "But just so you know, this isn't over. I won't rest again until I've made you scream my name in pleasure."

Prue swallowed thickly around the lump that instantly formed in her throat. There were no words that could be said with her body rioting out of control. She had no idea he was so dominant nor did she realize how turned on it made her.

She nodded and started down the path, leaving him to follow her. She simply couldn't look at him now in any capacity and stick to her plan.

CHAPTER

FIVE

Hours later they were deep in the woods and had turned up nothing. They'd covered nearly every inch of the island and teased each other mercilessly the whole way.

Now they were tired, hungry and horny as hell. At least she was for sure and not necessarily in that order. Brody had made the unilateral decision to take her to his small place for a much needed rest.

When they reached the cabin, Brody led her inside and locked the door behind them. She didn't even have time to survey her surroundings before he was on her again, this time picking her up with his hands under her thighs and encouraging her to wrap her legs around his waist.

She happily complied. He was already kissing her by the time they reached the bed and he lowered her, pressing her back into the mattress.

His lips were soft and firm as they traveled to her neck, and the small hollow above her collar bone. It was almost too much to believe that this hot, hard and beautiful man was solely focused on her.

He wanted her.

As if to emphasis his desire, his rough hands were exploring her curves at that very moment and every touch ignited new sparks that made her squirm.

"You have no idea how much I want you right now," he said, his lips still peppering kisses just above the curves of her breasts.

"Actually, I kind of do. I can feel how much pressing into my leg." She giggled, her lack of experience mixing with her need for him.

"You mean this?" He shifted his body so that his erection no longer rested on her leg and instead bumped the vee between her thighs.

She sucked in air at the sharp spike of need that shot through her. "Oh my God."

He chuckled before capturing her mouth for another deep kiss that robbed her of rational thought. He was hot, and so obviously into her that she had no trouble getting caught up in this inexplicable lust for a man she barely knew.

What did it matter if she gave in for once? At the moment she wanted him more than air. Her career? Forgotten for now. The needs she wanted to fulfill were far more basic and urgent than her first world problems.

Prue squirmed, unable to hold still under the onslaught of sensation coming from him.

"You are beautiful, Prue. Your reactions priceless. I'm not sure I can hold myself back much longer. I'm dying."

His words broke something inside her. The flimsy barrier that made her hold herself back.

Screw it.

She reached up and grabbed the back of his neck and slammed his lips back to hers at the same time lifting her hips to grind against him.

He growled into her mouth, while reaching for her right arm and pinning it above her head. He repeated just as swiftly with her left hand until she was pinned to the bed and they were both gasping with need with him clearly in control.

With his rough hands now entwined with hers that left only his mouth available to explore. Soft lips and hard hands all accompanied by growls and grunts worked together to turn her into a writhing mass of need.

"Show me what you like. I'm not sure what to do," she said.

"You're doing it," he said, his voice low and husky. "I touch, you respond. It's pure perfection."

He rolled his hips and her head nearly exploded. The friction he created at her center almost shot her off the bed. She wanted him so much she thought she'd die from it. The ache in her core kept growing the more he moved until she was thrashing against him.

It seemed the fact they were fully clothed didn't matter. He was hot, hard and lethal to her senses. She fought his hold, not because she didn't like the way he held her, but simply because instinct made her want to tear at something until the need inside her was sated.

"You're driving me crazy," she gasped.

"Good. I like crazy."

To her dismay, his thrusts slowed and some of the intensity inside her loosened. She was torn between crying from the loss of it and begging him to please not stop.

"Why are we stopping?" she asked.

"We aren't. Just prolonging the sensations a little longer." As soon as he got the words out, he moved between her thighs again in a long, slow stroke that reignited the fire in her core and made it burn even hotter than before.

"Oh my Gooooood," she crooned, her hips jerking against him.

Prue wasn't prepared for the sudden hunger Brody unleashed on her. But with the pure wave of pleasure that struck her nothing could have stopped it.

His movements were wild. His hands let go of her wrists and clawed at her clothes as he fought to liberate her from her shirt and bra. He must have been frustrated and stronger than she realized, because one second he was fighting her bra and the next it was ripped away from her.

"Stay there," he growled as he lifted himself off the bed.

She lifted her head and watched as he stripped his clothes, revealing hard abs with several beautiful ridges and a thick erection that made her eyes widen. A shudder of anticipation worked through her as he stared down at her with hungry eyes and an equally hungry expression stamped across his face.

"Are you sure about this, baby?" The gravelly sound of his voice vibrated across the bare skin of her stomach and made her nipples tighten. She whimpered.

Instead of trying to choke out words, she reached down and tugged at the button fastening her jeans. He stood silent watching her strip until she laid back down and placed her hands above her head, mimicking the motion of having him hold her down.

He groaned and licked his lips as he lowered to the foot of the bed, pressing his lips to her ankle.

"I wasn't kidding about wanting to taste every inch of you. Whether it takes all night or all week, it's my new goal."

His lips and hands blazed a trail up her legs causing sizzling sensations to ignite with every touch. The tight coil of pleasure began to form again in her center as he worked his way up her body.

"You smell so damned good," he groaned. His hands slid underneath her and cupped her bottom as he settled between her thighs, mouth poised inches from her sex.

Her stomach muscles tightened and her brain froze until he surprised her by sliding up and over her, his lips landing on her neck just below her ear.

The hard, heavy weight of his body comforted her—made her feel safe.

He didn't give her much time to think as he nibbled his way down her neck and chest before attaching his lips to one of her nipples, ripping a low groan from her dry throat.

The resulting riot of sensations flooded through her and went straight for her most vulnerable spots. Not that he stopped there. He trailed kisses to the next breast and captured the other nipple between his teeth. It was the sweetest torment she'd ever endured.

"You're driving me crazy," she gasped, her stomach muscles clenching in dizzying waves.

"Brody." His fingers digging at her hips added more heat to the firestorm inside her than she could bear. She needed more.

"I know, baby. I need it too." He lifted his chest and moved his hands between her legs where he massaged her folds. "So sweet and wet."

"I need more so bad it hurts," she whimpered.

"Then get ready for me to make it all better. Your pleasure is my pleasure, baby and I'm about to make you come."

He was working magic between her legs as he continued to tease her flesh. Using a combination of strong pressure and light, her body was ready to explode.

Vivid blue eyes tinged with so much gold it's all she saw, locked on her as his thumb swept across her clit.

She wanted to scream and couldn't, because her breath was trapped by the shock of pleasure overtaking her.

"Oh!" She dangled on the edge ready to succumb any second. Except...the pressure was easing.

"No. Please don't stop." She grabbed his arms and tried to push his hands back in position.

"Trust me, I'm not stopping." He settled his hips where his hands had been and she felt him pushing at her entrance. "Making it better, baby. Making you mine."

The steady pressure of him entering her made her cry out. Her muscles rippled around him as the pure overload of sensation made her body shake with hunger.

Oh dear God in heaven.

Nothing had ever felt like this before. Nothing. She thought it would hurt because he was so big, but she was so wet it worked out deliciously fine.

Before she could fully process all that was Brody making love to her, she was lifting her hips to meet his thrusts. They were both slick with sweat and the scent of sex surrounded them. Every detail imprinted on her brain to savor later.

Then her orgasm hit and everything fell away. One day or one year no longer mattered. In fact, she was pretty sure she was flat out screaming for more because her throat began to ache as Brody thrust several more times.

"Oh hell, Prue," he whispered. "You're making me come."

Pride made her body swell as he worked his hips at just the right angle to throw her into another explosion of pleasure. Her muscles clenched and this time everything froze. By the time she could breathe again, Brody collapsed on top of her, panting hard.

CHAPTER
SIX

Late into the night, Prue lay with her hand on Brody's chest, listening to his light snoring as he slept. A strange sense of peace had invaded her mind and she didn't know what to make of it. Her day had not gone at all like she'd planned or expected. Of course nothing could have prepared her for meeting Hurricane Brody. Like a storm, he'd somehow swept into her life and blown everything off course. All in a matter of hours.

Sometime between the first kiss in the woods to the latest orgasm in the small cabin, night had fallen along with her chance to finish her research.

In the morning she would have to return home empty handed. She glanced at the man lying beside her. Maybe if she moved quickly and quietly she could still find something...

Holding her breath she eased away from Brody and slid from the bed, taking care not to jostle the mattress more than absolutely necessary.

The first thing that hit her was the cool night air against her bare skin, thus reminding her she had no idea where her clothes were. She smiled. That's because when Brody finally got her here he couldn't get her clothes off fast enough. He'd practically torn them off. The memory made her shiver. That said, they had to be here somewhere.

She dropped to the floor and began feeling around. Of course the night she needed to see what the heck she was doing was the night of the new moon and no easy light to lead her way.

She twisted and turned, swiping her hand across the wood floor. About to give up she moved forward and collided with cloth.

Finally.

She grabbed her tank top and shoved it over her head. In light of her predicament, she could go without the bra she had no idea where it was.

In an awkward crab like walk she made her way around the room hands first until she came across her jeans. Once on, she stood and moved toward the door where her bag and shoes awaited. Minutes later she was ready to go and yet...

She turned back to Brody still sleeping on the bed. She so badly wanted to rejoin him. It would be so easy.

Except her research was important and her future depended on it. As amazing as he was in bed, she knew better than to turn a few hours of amazing sex into something more. Her world didn't work that way.

She slipped through the door and ignored the pain in her chest as she left him behind. This instant chemistry and attraction didn't make sense to her anyway. Sure science could explain a lot, but it didn't explain why it was hurting her to leave. Or why she suddenly wanted to make him hers for more than one night of orgasms.

Prue sighed. Time to shake it off.

Outside she turned left and headed for the thick woods behind the small cabin. More of the red berry blooms had to be around here somewhere.

Wind rustled through the trees, now surrounding her in a cloak of darkness. She dug through her bag and extracted the flashlight she packed into her gear before coming to the island. Another wave of nostalgia washed over her as the memory of her dad making sure she knew how to camp prepared for anything reminded her why she had the old light.

Focus, she reminded herself.

If she found the plants and returned the evidence to Wolf Haven then just maybe she could recover from the current disaster of her career.

She tromped through the dense brush and headed farther inland and away from the water. With the usual traffic around the water the wild berries had a better chance of survival in the opposite direction.

After what felt like forever of hiking up and down the uneven ground and hills, she stopped and dragged her sleeve across her forehead. Sweat was dripping down her face and getting into her eyes and her frustration was building with each fruitless moment.

"Stupid plants. Have to be here somewhere. I know it."

A rustle in the brush to her left startled her and Prue tripped, falling to the ground she tried to stop and failed before her knee slammed into a rock.

Pain exploded all around her as she continued to fall over the ledge of a small hill, rolling ass end over head to the bottom of a shallow ravine.

When she finally stopped she couldn't take a breath. Her chest ached as she grappled to recover from having the wind knocked out of her. Unable to move or function she was certain death had come for her.

Minutes that felt like hours passed before air trickled into her lungs again. Despite the pain coursing through her limbs she didn't move, only staring up at the inky star filled sky that she saw between the tall trees.

How far exactly had she fallen? Not just literally considering this had happened because she'd been obsessed with a plant that she thought might save her ass from unemployment.

Maybe it was time to accept defeat and reconsider a career change. This was ridiculous.

"Since you're breathing and not crying should I assume you're okay?"

A voice she didn't recognize came from the trail above her. Seriously? Busting her ass and failing miserably wasn't enough? Now she had to have an audience?

"Yeah, that's her. The woman Brody was supposed to keep an eye on."

Crap. Busted...

Prue remained still waiting for the two men to approach. One was one of the men from the beach although she couldn't remember his name for the life of her and the other she didn't recognize at all.

"Care to explain why you're snooping around my island in the dark, and in the middle of the night?" The unfamiliar man glared down at her.

"Research," she whispered, unsure of her voice still.

"Isn't that what you were supposed to finish up this afternoon?" This time the man from the beach questioned her.

A hot blush crept up her neck and face. "I—uh—got distracted and lost track of time. Since I have to leave in the morning I came out tonight for one last look around.

"And what did you find?"

She bit her lip and then answered. "Nothing." Wasn't that obvious at this point? She was flat on her ass with a scraped knee and various other aches and pains.

"Uh huh." The man she didn't know scooped her up under her arms and gently placed her on her feet.

"The important part is you're out here roaming the island in the middle of the night, unescorted. I believe my brother mentioned this is private property, yes?"

Prue suddenly felt like a child being scolded by a parent and it didn't sit well with her.

"Yes, but I don't think--"

He raised his hand and silenced her. "Please don't think, Ms. Davis, it's unbecoming. You *know* this is private property and you *know* that you were required to have an escort during your research. And yet, here you are alone with no one by your side to keep you safe."

She blinked, kind of stunned at this stranger's snide tone. Part of her wanted to give him a piece of her mind and the other wanted to crawl into a shell.

"I didn't catch your name, although I assume you are Diego's brother since you mentioned him. Either way, I really don't understand the big deal of me finding a plant or two. I had no intention of invading anyone's privacy and I certainly respect the wilderness and plan to leave it just as I found it."

To her irritation, he simply cocked an eyebrow at her while cocking his head towards the shrubbery she'd crashed into.

"Damien," he said.

She must have looked as confused as she felt.

"My name. And yes, Diego is my brother. And while I appreciate your obvious dedication to your work, I'm afraid I am going to have to ask you to leave." He turned to the man from the beach. "Creed, you'll make sure Ms. Davis is escorted off the island."

"What about Brody?" Creed asked.

Damien frowned. "I think we've indulged Mr. Fox long enough. I've tolerated him because of Diego, but I think enough is enough. Ms. Davis has to go."

Before she could form a decent response, Damien had disappeared into the darkness and only she and Creed still stood in the clearing.

"What the hell was that all about?" she asked.

"Damien can be prickly. Especially when it comes to his mate."

"Mate?" She scrunched up her face. Why in the world would anyone refer to their girlfriend or wife as a mate?

"Wife. Whatever." Creed looked down at her. "Do you need some help? My jeep is just at the end of this trail if you're up to walking."

"I do not need help walking." Nor did she need these overbearing pains in the asses telling her what to do every two seconds. They were worse than the stuffy know it alls at the university.

Creed held up his hands. "No sweat, Professor. I'm just doing my job."

"Why does everyone keep calling me a Professor? I'm not, okay? And by job what exactly do you mean? How am I a part of your job?"

"You heard the boss man. I'm escorting you out of here." He indicated the path in front of him. "After you."

"What about Brody? Will we see him before I'm thrown off the island in the middle of the night? I didn't exactly tell him I was leaving."

"I figured as much. Or at least I hoped that was the case. You were a test for him and while he kind of failed, I think there might still be hope for him."

She stopped walking and turned back to Creed. "I have no idea what any of that means. Why would I be a test for anyone?"

Creed laughed, a low and dark sound that didn't exactly sound joyful. In fact, it kind of scared the hell out of her. "Doesn't matter anymore. Times up."

SEVEN

"What do you mean she's gone? Where the hell did she go?" Brody could barely contain his fury at the thought of his mate having left the island without him. Unclaimed and unaware put her in a very dangerous position if she encountered another shifter. "Sun's not even up yet."

"That's why I'm here." Sawyer, another one of the pack security guards, wisely took a few steps away from Brody. "The alphas had her ejected from the island not long ago after they found her snooping alone in the woods. I thought you might want to know."

He grabbed his jeans and shoved his legs into them. "Information that might have been useful before she was gone. Now I've got to go after her."

"I know you've got to do what you've got to do, bro. But leaving right now might not fare well for you. Damien is probably crawling up Diego's ass right now over you."

He slid his feet into his boots and laced up. Quickly followed by the dark T-shirt he'd had on earlier.

"I don't give a shit about Damien or Diego or anyone else right now for that matter. She's mine and she belongs with me."

Sawyer smiled. "Figured as much. Creed is always right about these things, but shit, better you than me. This situation is getting complicated."

"I don't see why. You all keep telling me this mate shit is mystical and all-powerful. She's obviously not the first human, so what's the big deal?"

"Dude, it's not mating season. It's not supposed to happen like this. You should be able to control it. The fact you can't is scaring everyone. It makes you dangerous."

Brody leaned forward, a twisted smile spreading across his face. "You all should have thought about that before you took my mate away from me. If I don't find her or anything has happened to her, this place is going to burn."

Sawyer took a step forward, anger twisting his face. "Don't threaten me or our pack. I came here to help you so back the fuck off. I might give you a pass once, but it's not going to happen again. You feel me?"

Brody took a deep breath, wishing it would calm him. His need for Prue had him all twisted up inside. "Yeah I got it. But it doesn't change the fact of who I hold responsible for her safety right now."

"Yeah, about that. How the hell was she out there alone? A human got the drop on you?" Sawyer shook his head. "Our training doesn't seem to be working."

Brody tightened his hands into fists as he stalked to the front door. "Oh it worked. Trust me. It worked."

He slammed the door open and rushed through it. "Key!" he yelled back at Sawyer.

"Nope. You're not leaving me behind and this is my truck. I'm the only one who drives her."

Brody rolled his eyes and climbed into the cab of Sawyer's vehicular baby. "Where did Creed take her?"

He shrugged. "Not sure. Her car was parked on the other side of the bridge where most visitors have to park, but he wouldn't have just dropped her there. He would have followed her out of town at least. Probably across the big bridge to make sure she didn't hang around the peninsula."

"She lives in Montana. But she was trying to get her research for Wolf Haven. That's my bet on the first place she'd go. I don't think she's prepared to return home empty handed."

Sawyer shook his head and headed off the island. They weren't a mile off the island when Brody spotted her silver compact tucked in some trees in the parking area at the nearby state park.

"What the hell?" Sawyer swerved across the road and entered through the gate. "Someone's more determined than we gave her credit for."

Brody jumped from the truck before Sawyer slammed it into park and took off in the direction of the beach. For the first time since Sawyer woke him by pounding on his front door, he let some of his rigid control slip and let the wolf join the hunt. He needed the extra senses to save time.

It didn't take him long to sift through the various human scents to find her distinctive wild and sweet scent. The wolf growled and he agreed. His instincts screamed to hurry.

He tore through the trail and down several sets of stairs that led him down the edge of the coast until he burst through the trees.

Fifty yards down the sand stood his mate. She'd stripped down to shorts and a tank top and his body stiffened all over at the sight of her lush body that had been in his bed just hours before. He heard her screams of ecstasy all over again in his head and made note to make that happen again as soon as possible.

When she began walking into the water, he called out. "Prue! Stop!"

She turned at the sound of his voice and her eyes widened. He growled in response, while stalking forward.

"What the hell, woman. Why are you out here instead of still in my bed where you belong?"

"Excuse me? Where I belong? What is that supposed to mean?"

Finally close enough to reach her he wrapped his arms around her and tugged her against his front. "Exactly as it sounds. You belong in my bed."

"But—I—you should probably tell that to your friends. I was escorted off the island."

"Yeah, I heard you were out snooping through the island on your own. You should have woken me."

She frowned, her lips pursing. "I was not snooping! I was simply trying to find my plants. I seriously do not understand why everyone is making such a big deal out of that. In fact I would think that if your island has a plant infestation that is luring wild wolves to the area you'd appreciate someone like me solving that problem before someone gets hurt."

He nodded. "Speaking of that. We need to talk. I was hoping to have this conversation after a few more orgasms, but I guess that's not the way it's meant to go down."

Her mouth dropped open and he took that opportunity to swoop forward and capture her with a kiss. Time to remind her how insane they sizzled together.

"Well, well. What do we have here?"

They broke free from the kiss and Brody whirled to the familiar unfriendly voice, shoving Prue behind him. His uncle on his father's side stood less than ten feet away. Two more men behind him with sawed off shotguns pointed in the direction of him and Prue.

"What the hell are you doing here?" he demanded, keeping his eye on the men *and* their weapons.

"I guess I could ask you the same thing, but I think we both already know the answer."

Brody's body vibrated from tension as he surveyed the area behind his uncle.

"He's fine for now. Two of your cousins are currently detaining your friend back at his truck. Feisty that one. Hope he doesn't try anything crazy."

"You're asking for more trouble than you know by coming here. How did you find me? No, never mind. It doesn't matter. You should leave before the others figure out you're here." Not that he believed for even a second that his uncle would just walk away or tell him the truth.

"Brody, what's going on?" Prue tried to walk around him and he forced her behind his back.

"Stay still, babe. I need to finish this."

"She yours now?" his uncle asked. "She's been very helpful in our investigation and led us straight to your front door."

Brody growled, baring his teeth. "You don't know what you're talking about, old man."

His face twisted into a smug grin. "Oh I think I do. Doc here reports there's an island with an unusual number of wolf sightings. I don't need science to tell me what's happening. I know exactly what's going on. We've got ourselves another infestation of nasty shapeshifters. That's what is going on."

"Whaaaat?" Prue said, behind him.

"Oh have you not told her?" His uncle chuckled. "My bad."

"Shut up," Brody roared, the haze of red returning to his vision. His control was slipping faster than he could contain it. Shit. This was not how he wanted her to discover his secret.

"You have no rights in this family anymore, Brody boy. You're one of them now. That means you'll die with the rest of them right here in front of your pretty new girlfriend. I sure hope you were kind enough to use a condom when you fucked her. Forcing your pups on her would be cruel and unusual, especially when they turned and had to be killed."

Brody exploded at the same time Prue gasped behind him. "You son of a—" Hair burst through his skin and muscles and bones popped causing extreme pain that he ignored thanks to the overdose of adrenalin pumping through him.

The only thing that registered were the sounds of his clothes ripping and the wolf wresting him for control.

"Jesus Chr—" His uncle's words died in the wind as Brody jumped on his chest and slammed him to the ground. He rolled, pulling his prey with him and using his body as a shield from the men with guns.

A howl broke the silence and Brody turned in the direction of Sawyer's truck. A large gray wolf bounded toward him and the two men swiveled in his direction.

"Put your guns down now or I rip his throat out," Brody growled, regaining their attention. To emphasize his intent, he slid his claws through the flesh of his uncle's neck, drawing blood and making it clear how vulnerable the man's throat was.

His agonizing moan helped too. The two men froze and looked at each other. Sawyer partially shifted from wolf keeping his claws and fangs as he approached them.

"Brody, don't do this. Don't kill him. You can't come back from that."

Prue's worried voice penetrated his thoughts. She didn't understand what was at stake here.

"They already know too much. If we let them go it puts the whole pack at risk."

She jumped forward and grasped his shirt. "There has to be another way."

He could hear the fear in her voice and he didn't like it. He wanted to end this the only way he knew how—with blood.

"He's right. Alive these men will never keep their mouths shut."

"Can't you just capture them? Maybe they could be useful for information or something," Prue argued.

Brody traded glances with Sawyer who shrugged his shoulders.

"Maybe," he said. "If nothing else Dante could decide their fate."

Brody tightened his grip around his uncle's neck as he keened in agony. It went against everything he believed in to let them go. If anyone knew his family like he did they would certainly agree.

As if to take the decision out of his hands, Sawyer grabbed the guns from the other two men and threw them into the ocean. "Only pussies need guns."

"Fuck you." One of the men made the mistake of spitting in Sawyer's face. Brody held his breath for a second.

"Prue, get the fuck behind me right now!"

"Why?" She turned back to Sawyer who was circling his prey.

"Prue!" he yelled, deepening his tone.

Thank God his message got through when she stomped through the sand until she was a safe distance away and no longer in between him and the rest of the hunters.

"What's it going to be boys? You going to cooperate or am I going to gut him?"

Brody's uncle grunted at the question, his only option with claws piercing his vocal chords.

"We aren't doing shit for wolves. Go ahead and kill him. You'll have the entire community so far up your ass before you can say thank you."

Brody growled, his claws moving slowly through vulnerable flesh.

"Brody no!" Prue screamed. Distracted, he turned to check on his mate, giving the hunters the split second they needed to attack.

He saw Prue scream a millimeter before a steel toed boot connected with his head. His grip on his uncle loosened enough for him to yank free without losing his throat.

Brody's head exploded in pain and he fell face first in the sand. In the seconds it took him to regain his equilibrium, the two hunters attacked Sawyer and the three of them were fighting to the death.

His uncle on the other hand, he knew the exact way to take Brody down and it had nothing to do with killing him. The bastard went after Prue, grabbing her by the hair and spinning her around until the knife he seemingly pulled out of thin air rested at her throat.

"Another inch and she bleeds out on the beach." The hoarse, sand paper sound of his uncle's voice sent him over the edge. Between the blood flowing from the man's neck and the torn vocal chords, he was already dead and Brody would be damned before he allowed him to take Prue along for the ride.

"Let her go."

"Or what? You'll kill me? That ship has sailed, but I can do this one last thing before I go. Payback is a bitch isn't it?"

CHAPTER

EIGHT

The blade dug into Prue's skin and the fear flooding her senses morphed into determination. She was not going to die like this.

In a lightning move that called on every self defense class she'd ever taken, she slammed her forearm against the arm wielding the knife and knocked it away just long enough to swing her arm up and shove the palm of her hand up into the old man's chin.

It only bought her a few seconds but it gave her the chance to turn and run and enough time for Brody to reach them. With her back to the fighting she ran as fast as her out of shape legs would allow, ignoring the snarls and sounds of the men behind her.

Violence like this had only been in her life once and it felt eerily similar. Except the man coming to her rescue was the animal versus the other way around.

When she heard a sharp crack, she fell to the sand immobilized by the assault of memories of the bear mauling her father to death in front of her. The blood and screams of her father telling her to run as loud today as they were then.

She covered her ears and tried to wipe the sound from her mind. But she knew better. Nothing ever could take it away. Death never went away.

"Prue, baby, it's okay. You're safe." Arms were trying to wrap around her and lift her from the ball she'd curled into and she wanted none of it. She fought and kicked and punched until Brody released her and backed off.

"Prue, Goddammit. Calm down. You're safe."

"Am I?" she fired back. "You're not human, Brody. That's not normal."

He dropped down in the sand next to her and blew out a hard breath. "I know. Believe me I know. For your sake I wish I was normal."

Silence ensued as they both sat there staring out at the water. The wind coming in dried the tears on her face and a new calm wrapped around her once again. "A bear mauled my father to death when I was a teenager and even though years have passed, I'm never going to get over it. And now I'm scared all over again."

"You're scared of me."

It wasn't a question and even if it was she didn't know how to answer it so she stayed silent.

Brody took a deep breath and exhaled hard. She could have sworn she heard the sound of defeat.

"Six months ago I was as human as you are. I didn't ask for this. I had a different life in a different place. It might not have been the best of times but it was familiar and I thought I was happy."

Prue turned her head and watched him from underneath the hair that tumbled across her glasses. The ferocious wolf shifter she'd seen minutes ago had given way to a vulnerable man telling her his story. She had to listen. No, she wanted to hear it.

"What happened?" she asked.

"My family hunts down shapeshifters and kills them. They do this because they believe that they are demonic and dirty or any other biblical nonsense they can come up with. We didn't understand them or even try. So we killed what we feared."

Prue shuddered at the idea of the violence that Brody had been born into.

"I'm not going to lie to you. I have a lot of blood on my hands. As sick as that makes me, it's the truth. There is nothing I can say or do to take that back. But it's not who I am anymore. The last wolf I confronted was a lot more powerful than I expected. Eventually I gained the upper hand, but the moment he realized he couldn't beat me he decided to teach me a lesson and bit me."

She gasped. "He bit you and turned you into a wolf. That's really all it takes? A bite?"

"The answer to that is surprisingly complicated. Yes and no. The rules are apparently fluid based on Mother Nature's whim. As I understand it, during mating season in the spring, a human can be turned under the right conditions. i.e. a bond is formed and hell, I don't understand it at all actually."

Prue sat up, fascinated by the science of such a thing. "But that's not what happened to you."

"Nope and supposedly the bite I got should have killed me. So there are a lot of unanswered questions that even the pack doesn't know. Much of their history was lost over the years so they sometimes make it up as they go. For example, they aren't allowed to go around biting people on a whim. There are repercussions for that kind of thing."

"So if you bit me right now, I would likely die?"She scooted several feet down the sand.

"I would never hurt you. I have to protect you."

She scrunched up her face, confused. "Why do you *have* to protect me?"

"Because the wolf has claimed you as its mate."

Prue opened and shut her mouth several times. She was so stunned she didn't know what to say. She jumped to her feet and crossed her arms over her chest.

"Claim me? You can't claim me. I am an independent woman. A *human* one. I don't get claimed."

"You do have the right to reject it. I'm not going to force you into anything you don't want."

Her shoulders relaxed a fraction. "Thank God."

"This isn't how I wanted you to find out. I thought we'd have more time to get to know each other before you learned the truth. But either way, what happens next is your choice not mine."

Then why did he sound so forlorn? He sounded like all of his hopes and dreams had just been crushed.

"Brody, what happens to the wolf if I reject the claim?" She remembered some scientific research that suggested that real wolves who lost their mate never fully recovered from that loss.

He shrugged. "Not totally sure. I'm new at this too. Although I do know Creed's mate rejected him and he's one cranky ass bastard most of the time."

She flounced onto the sand again, torn between the part of her brain that told her to get the hell out of there as fast as she could and the other that remembered every second with Brody in minute exquisite detail.

Especially the multiple orgasm parts...

God, really? She grabbed her head. What the hell was wrong with her? How can the sex be in her mind now? Now she really knew the crazy was setting in.

"Uhm... Prue?"

"What?" she asked without looking up.

"We haven't talked about this yet, but I have the heightened senses of the wolf at all times."

"Okaaay." She didn't know why that was important right now other than it was good to know interesting data.

"That means I can smell things most people can't." He hesitated. "Like arousal. And in your case it compels me to do something about it."

It took a few seconds until his words sank in...

She jumped to her feet and whirled to face him again only to find him standing as well.

She planted her hand on her hip and glared at a very naked and very aroused Brody. "I think you have some explaining to do."

"I thought you deserved to know." He stalked toward her.

"Stop right there. I need to process this. But I can't wrap my mind around it."

"I'm still the man you've been with since yesterday. This doesn't change anything I've said."

"And the wolf?" she asked. "That was you on the beach last spring, wasn't it?"

He nodded. "I followed you after I caught your scent. We were both drawn to you."

"Is that all this is about? You're horny because the wolf wants to mate?"

He rolled his eyes. "Still human too, babe. I have some control, but I can't help it if my body and wolf responds to your arousal."

She dropped down onto a nearby rock and rubbed her hands across her thighs. "I guess this explains why the word mate kept coming up in conversations with your friends. It's a wolf thing." She lifted her head. "Are they all wolves? Your sister too?"

"Yes. Allison met Diego and one thing led to another. It was mating season, they connected on a primal level and I guess on a human level too and next thing I knew she was being turned after being claimed by Diego and his pack."

"Oh my God this is insane. Am I about to wake up from a strange dream?"

"Do you want to?"

Prue lifted her head and found him staring at her with a sadness that she felt bone deep. If she woke up from all of this then that would mean Brody wasn't real and she was pretty sure that would break her heart in two.

"I'm a biologist. This kind of discovery should be a scientist's dream."

His frown deepened and his shoulders stiffened. "Of course. I'm sure the opportunity to study me must be an incredible coup."

She shook her head. "But my first thought was of you, the man. Not the wolf or the wolves of your pack. Whatever happens, I don't want to unknow you. I don't want to forget our night in your cabin and I sure as hell don't want to lose these feelings that are growing at lightning speed. No matter how much this all confuses me. I don't want to lose you."

He closed the space between them before she could take a breath. "That's all I needed to hear." He tucked her hair behind her ear. "I know this is happening fast, it is for me too. We can do this together and learn all about the future before any irrevocable decisions have to be made. But I already know this. You. Are. Mine."

Brody leaned forward and covered her mouth, sweeping his tongue inside to fully claim what he wanted. Her reservations melted as she sank into his kiss. If going fast and feeling crazy meant she had more of him and this, then sign her up.

The rest she'd figure out later.

"If I am yours then that makes you mine."

Brody growled, making that low rumble in this throat that made her legs get weak and her panties get wet.

She growled back, mimicking the sound he made.

His hands grabbed her hips and squeezed. "You're making me crazy, woman.

"Then I guess I've joined the club.

EPILOGUE

The table was set, the candles were lit and the steaks were ready for the grill. Brody wasn't sure about this romance thing, but Allison had convinced him this was the way to go.

Except Prue was naked in the bathtub without him, and it was killing him. The thought of her naked body wet and covered in bubbles from her bath made him tight all over.

Everything between them had happened so fast, there were times he hardly believed it. Of course the mate thing pushed him to her, but it was everything about her that kept the man wanting more. He couldn't get enough. Now he wanted to make this permanent, but without the force of a mating. He wanted her to choose him. To choose to stay with him forever.

"Screw this." He grabbed the bottle of wine and two glasses and headed into the bathroom he'd built especially for her into their small cabin.

She'd insisted that they needed to stay here for now, but missed soaking in a bath. So he added one. It was the least he could do for the woman who surprised him day in and day out with her thirst for knowledge and unqualified acceptance of who and what he was.

He opened the door and inhaled, taking in the sexy scent of his woman that now mingled with her lavender scented bubble bath. From the doorway he saw her sexy, strong legs poking out of the white suds, making him think of what it felt like to have them wrapped around his waist as he sank into her.

He groaned.

"Hey! I thought you were giving me some private time tonight."

He stalked forward, wholly intent on getting inside her. "I did. And then I couldn't stop thinking about you naked in here and covered in frothy white bubbles. I got tired of waiting. A man can only take so much you know."

"Maybe I'm worn out. Marathon sex with a hot guy like you can take a real toll."

He stopped walking, concern replacing need. "Are you okay? Have I hurt you? That was never my intention. I cherish you. It's just, I don't know. I can't keep away."

The corners of her mouth quirked moments before she broke into a huge grin. "Oh my God, I was kidding! You are too easy."

While relief swept through him, he frowned and moved forward, stopping at the edge of her porcelain tub and placing the wine and glasses on the floor.

"Just for that..." He lifted her from the tub and stepped in behind her. He then spun her around before settling her against him chest to chest.

"You feel happy to see me." She tried to continue joking with him, but he heard the husky need in every syllable. Her skin was flushed and the dark points of her lush breasts made it clear she was as needy as he was.

"Smart ass." He didn't wait for her next comeback. He leaned forward and kissed her, hopefully searing them both to their soul. They weren't yet officially mated, and wouldn't be until next spring, but he swore the bond was already there. It held him in thrall every day.

With her scent teasing him in every way, he reached for her leg and bent it out of the way so he could slide inside her.

Ahhhh.

Sometimes he enjoyed taking her slow, but this wasn't one of those moments. He groaned as he grabbed her waist and dragged her up and then pushed her back down. He'd wanted Prue from the moment he scented her and nothing had changed.

Hopefully feeling as frantic as him, she took up his rhythm and moved them faster and faster, while water sloshed from the tub. Neither stayed quiet either. One of the reasons they stayed this far out from the others in the tiny cabin.

Prue threaded her fingers into his hair and tugged, not at all gentle. Normally he preferred to be in charge, but he'd learned with his mate, letting go was as powerful as being in control.

Prue's cries grew louder as he frantically held on. One last thrust inside her and the love of his life came apart in his arms.

Beautiful and exquisite.

The joy filling his heart as he came with her nearly broke him. Her cries, his shouts, they all mingled together in a primal declaration that no words needed to convey. All doubts were erased and in his mind they were already mated.

"Mine," he growled, breathless.

She simply lifted her head from his shoulder and pressed a soft kiss to his mouth, her eyes dreamy with pleasure.

"No," she panted. "Mine."

He grinned. She was going to make one hell of a wolf.

DAMIEN EASED the door to the greenhouse open and walked in. He found Dante hunched over a row of Devil's Club extracting the oil from its roots, the secret ingredient in their island distilled whiskey of the same name.

"Hard at work I see."

Dante didn't look up. "Someone's got to do it. Not all of us have the luxury of standing around Club Diablo and checking out women."

Damien scoffed. "Yeah, you're hilarious. Don't let Faith hear you say shit like that or there will be blows."

"So what brings you down here tonight? Club business not going well?"

Damien poked at one of the berry covered flower heads. "Business is as usual." He didn't elaborate beyond that. The club had normal weekend business and no other hunter incidents had occurred since the confrontation Brody had with his family at the beach a few weeks prior.

Dante straightened and focused his attention toward him instead of the plants they grew only in this greenhouse. "So what is it then? This isn't one of your usual hangouts."

"Something is still off and I'm waiting for the other shoe to drop. I doubt we've seen the last of the hunters. It seems taking in Allison and Brody is proving to be as dangerous as I suspected."

Dante snorted. "I would have liked to have seen you try to take Allison away from Diego. I could have sold tickets to that show."

He ignored his brother's sarcasm. He wasn't in the mood. "Ms. Davis is still a wild card. I believe she didn't intentionally help the hunters find us, but that doesn't mean she won't in the future. Not to mention she still keeps trying to find this stupid plant on the island."

"Only until the next mating season when Brody can turn her. Although to watch the two of them now seems no different than us with our mates. With her by his side his entire attitude and demeanor have changed. As for the plant, is it really going to hurt anyone to find out?"

He shrugged. "Something's coming, I can feel it. It's keeping me up at night."

"Maybe you need to spend more time with Faith and less time at work. It's getting to your brain. Or you could do this and I could go home to Ruby."

Maybe Dante was right and maybe he wasn't. The fact they kept their greenhouse ingredient a secret wasn't that big of a deal. Except he didn't trust outsiders and like it or not they had three too many right now. If the situation were to ever spiral out of control...

He fingered one of the plants until a thick thorn broke through his skin and blood poured from the tiny hole. "Mark my words, little brother. One way or another trouble is headed our way.

———✕◦◖◉◗◦✕———

Thank you so much for reading!

READY TO CONTINUE with more Devils Point Wolves? Creed, the head of pack security, is about to have more than he bargained for on his hands and she is keeping one hell of a secret.

Please look for **FIERCE**, available now.

Join Eliza's VIP newsletter at elizagayle.com/newsletter and be the first to be notified of new releases, sales and contests.

Continue reading for an extended excerpt from FIERCE, the next book in the Devils Point Wolves series and the full booklist from Eliza Gayle.

If you enjoyed this story please take a moment to help other readers discover it by leaving a review on your favorite retailer.

Just a few words and some stars really does help

SNEAK PEEK FROM FIERCE

FIERCE

By Eliza Gayle
Copyright 2016
All Rights Reserved

Book Description:

Don't mess with mama...

Creed Donovan hates being alone.

Fortunately for him there is no shortage of women who like a man with a dark side and the attitude to match. He'll never take a mate because he already has one. She just wants nothing to do with him or his kind. Except on payday at Club Diablo where she struts her body seven nights a week for any man with cash.

Except him. Because he hasn't set foot inside the pack club since she rejected him. It wouldn't do for the head of pack security to be the one ripping out a man's throat for looking the wrong way at his mate.

Dani's life is one mistake after another.

First, she's got medical bills stacking up and needs money now, but her time as an exotic dancer has an early expiration date and it's coming soon. Extra shifts for as long as she can get them are a no brainer. Which leads to the second issue.

She's tired of reliving the pain of her broken would-be relationship with Creed every time she steps foot on Devils Point. Add to that her feet hurt all the time and her body is no longer her friend. Especially when it aches to have Creed touch her again.

She can't deny her taste for a certain bad boy, but the past has to stay in the past. No matter how good he smells.

Chapter One

Creed leaned against his motorcycle and took a deep drag of his cigarette. Standing here staring at the entrance of Club Diablo had been a really bad idea. Even if he was simply waiting on Sawyer to arrive for their nightly debrief.

He was pretty sure the bastard was trying to torture him, although he didn't know why. Creed turned his head and looked at the bright red convertible that belonged to Dani, or Melody, the stage name most of the club knew her by, the bane of his existence and the woman he wanted more than air every single hour of the day.

That she came to work seven nights a week on his island while she ignored him burned his ass more and more each passing day.

Fucking bullshit.

He had half a mind to march inside and take what was his whether she liked it or not. Anger brewed inside him alongside the desire. Together they were a lethal combination as far as he was concerned.

It made him imagine her curves strutting across the stage, her hands running alongside her sweet skin, drawing all the attention right where she wanted it. On her and her perfectly luscious body.

She was damned good at her job and got paid ridiculously well for it. There was little doubt how many men flocked to the club to see their most popular dancer.

His eyes slid closed on the image of her licking her cherry red pouty lips, her blonde hair sleek and straight falling down to the tiny waist that flared into full hips that gave him more than enough to hold onto as he pushed inside her.

Creed growled, his eyes jerking open. Great. Now his dick was hard and aching again. A few minutes more of this damned train of thought and Sawyer would arrive to find him jacking off to relieve the pressure.

He reached down and adjusted, trying to find more room in his now snug jeans. Sawyer had thirty seconds to get his ass in this parking lot or he was leaving. There was a bar filled with eager women in nearby Tacoma waiting for the opportunity to relieve his stress and he was fucking ready.

After one last drag on the cigarette still dangling from his lips, Creed threw the butt down and ground it out with his boot.

A low rumble of a modified SUV sounded behind him, alerting him that his packmate and fellow security sentinel, Sawyer, had finally arrived. With his headlights turned off, his friend circled the parking lot and pulled in next to him. His window slid down and Creed had the sudden urge to wipe the smug, knowing smile from Sawyer's face.

"Let's get this over with," he growled. "Got somewhere to be."

"Another new one? What does that make? Three this week?"

He shrugged, not caring for the condemnation in his voice. What the hell did he know? He still hoped to find his mate.

Only because he had no idea how painful it was both physically and mentally to be rejected by one. If Sawyer really understood he wouldn't be so eager to keep looking.

"How's the north end? Any activity to report?"

Sawyer shook his head. "All quiet and everyone accounted for."

Creed nodded his head. "Same on the south end. It's making me nervous though. It has been too long. Something should have happened. I don't believe the hunters are going to let the disappearance of their men go."

"Be grateful, man. If the bastards haven't figured out what happened to them by now they probably never will. Assholes must have come here on their own and not told anyone."

Creed pressed his lips together in a deep frown. Maybe...

Except he didn't like it one bit. Brody and Allison had given them enough information for them to know these hunters were organized and retaliation likely. So where the hell were they hiding?

"I hope you're right." He grabbed the back of his neck and rubbed. "Can't shake the feeling something is going to happen."

Sawyer grinned at him. "You're wound so tight you can't see straight, dude, and it has nothing to do with hunters. When are you going to do something about her?"

Creed didn't bother pretending he didn't know exactly what his friend was talking about. There was some truth in the fact she had him in knots.

"I'm not into forcing women. No means no."

Sawyer waited half a heartbeat before he started laughing at him. "You're an idiot, you know that?"

"Whatever. I'm out of here." Creed put on his helmet and mounted his waiting bike.

"You sure you don't want to go in with me? The club could use you. And I think there's something you should see for yourself."

Creed shook his head. Going in now, with the need for her nearly choking him, would not bode well for anyone. "You've got this. I'll see you tomorrow."

He cranked up his engine before Sawyer could give him any more good reasons to go inside. The mood he was in did not make it easy. But for Melody's sake and his, he stayed away. He would accept for now that she wanted to live her life without him.

With a twist of his wrist he gunned the engine and started toward the bridge, seeking the freedom he needed right now.

In his rearview mirror he spied Sawyer slipping through the front door of the club. He did want to join him, a lot more than he wanted empty comfort from others. What he wasn't in the mood for was the fiftieth rejection from Miss Hot Shot stripper.

He was done. His pride would allow no more groveling.

Bitterness flooded through him as he rushed off the island and toward the mainland. He was beyond ready to do whatever it took to get over her.

No sooner did his wheels hit the bridge before his entire world exploded behind him, a blast of heat and light flinging him and his bike sideways into the concrete and metal guardrails.

In a strange slow motion, Creed tried to get out from underneath the hunk of metal. Pain shot from his leg and side as he maneuvered free. The night had gone from gloomy and dark to hot and bright in a matter of seconds and he had no idea what had happened.

He limped from the edge of the road, the sound of metal grinding against metal still ringing in his ears, and turned back toward the island. He stood transfixed as the horror of what he saw before him began to sink in. A wall of flames surrounded Club Diablo with a rain of burning debris littering the night sky as it fell to the ground.

What the fuck?

Mate. The wolf rasped in his head.

Creed jerked, moving on autopilot as he began ripping at his clothes while his bones popped and muscles strained as the change to wolf overtook him. The human in him receded and the animal seized control.

One minute he was standing by the road in pain and the next the wolf was racing across the bridge to the burning building with only one goal in mind.

Save the mate.

The closer he got the harder his heart hammered. The buzzing in his head got louder too. Smoke billowed into the parking lot making it harder to see as he sprinted the last fifty yards to the building. Damien stood close to the front door barking orders as he dragged one of the customers from the building. There were several people staggering around the parking lot, but Creed didn't spot Dani anywhere.

The fist holding his heart in its hand squeezed harder. She had to be okay.

Had. To. Be.

Read more now in Fierce, now available.

ALSO BY ELIZA GAYLE

The Dragon Lore Trilogy:

THE CURSE OF THE DRAGON

THE SOUL OF THE DRAGON

THE FIRE OF THE DRAGON

Southern Shifters Series:

SHIFTER MARKED

MATE NIGHT

ALPHA KNOWS BEST

BAD KITTY

BE WERE

SHIFTIN' DIRTY

BEAR NAKED TRUTH

ALPHA BEAST

ONE CRAZY WOLF

Enigma Shifters Fated Mates:

DRAGON MATED

WOLF BAITED

BEARLY DATED

WOLF TEMPTED

Devils Point Wolves:

WILD

WICKED

WANTED

FERAL

FIERCE

FURY

Single titles:

VAMPIRE AWAKENING

WITCH AND WERE

WRITING AS E.M. GAYLE
CONTEMPORARY ROMANCE

Mafia Mayhem Duet Series:

MERCILESS SINNER

SINNER TAKES ALL

WICKED BEAST

WILLING BEAUTY

BROKEN SAINT

FALLEN ANGEL

Outlaw Justice Series:

SAVAGE PROTECTOR

RECKLESS PAWN

RUTHLESS REDEMPTION

Outlaw Justice: Sins of Wrath MC:

CRUEL SAVIOR

SCORCHED KING

VICIOUS DEFENDER

Purgatory Masters Series:

TUCKER'S FALL

LEVI'S ULTIMATUM

MASON'S RULE

GABE'S OBSESSION

GABE'S RECKONING

Purgatory Club:

ROPED

WATCH ME

TEASED

BURN

BOTTOMS UP

HOLD ME CLOSE

Pleasure Playground Series:

PLAY WITH ME

POWER PLAY

Single Title:

TAMING BEAUTY

WICKED CHRISTMAS EVE

9 798215 807330